WICKED WARRIOR

Tales of a Terrarian Warrior, Book Three

WICKED WARRIOR

AN UNOFFICIAL TERRARIAN WARRIOR NOVEL

WINTER MORGAN

Sky Pony Press
New York

Sky Pony Press books may be purchased in bulk at special discounts for sales promotion, corporate gifts, fund-raising, or educational purposes. Special editions can also be created to specifications. For details, contact the Special Sales Department, Sky Pony Press, 307 West 36th Street, 11th Floor, New York, NY 10018 or info@skyhorsepublishing.com.

Sky Pony® is a registered trademark of Skyhorse Publishing, Inc.®, a Delaware corporation.

Visit our website at www.skyponypress.com.

10 9 8 7 6 5 4 3 2 1

Library of Congress Cataloging-in-Publication Data is available on file.

Cover design by Brian Peterson
Cover illustration by Amanda Bracken

Print ISBN: 978-1-5107-2195-1
Ebook ISBN: 978-1-5107-2197-5

Printed in Canada

TABLE OF CONTENTS

WICKED WARRIOR

Chapter 1:
FOLLOW THE INSTRUCTIONS

Miles looked back at the village and stared at the setting sun casting its last sliver of light onto the rooftops. He could hear the muffled hum of his friends' voices in the distance. Miles was annoyed at himself, because he had just left, and homesickness was already setting in. He recalled Sarah lovingly cutting his hair and John gifting him a potion of healing, and he missed them both. Miles expected he'd crave the comforts of home, and knew there were many sacrifices involved in becoming a warrior, but he hadn't expected to be this heartbroken about leaving. The sunset and darkness settled in. Miles took a deep breath, as two zombies spawned in the distance. He wanted to sprint back to his house, but he knew he must face this challenge.

Grabbing armor from his inventory, Miles proceeded, striking one of the zombies with a sword.

The zombie jumped, missing the blow, and lunged toward Miles. Using all of his might, Miles struck the zombie repeatedly, destroying it while dodging an attack from the other zombie. With a final strike from his sword, Miles destroyed the second zombie. He picked up the drops, a shackle and zombie arm that they had dropped on the ground, and placed both rewards in his inventory.

Fresh from his victory over this undead mob of the night, Miles felt confident that he would be able to defeat The Destroyer. He paused, scanning the distance for any other hostile mobs that lurked in the thick of the night. Miles had to stay focused and strategize the best ways to defeat lethal mobs, while constantly looking for ones that might surprise him. He turned in all directions, taking one last look back at the village and although nobody could hear him, he called out, "Goodbye friends. I promise to make you proud. I will defeat The Destroyer."

Before he left, Isabella had said, "Miles, I can't wait to hear all of your tales about slaying impossible beasts when you return home as a hero."

Even Cedric the wizard believed in Miles, telling him in a rather lengthy monologue that he was certainly sure Miles would achieve ultimate success in Terraria and would return home with a Buckets of Bolts achievement. "You will achieve greatness, my friend. I look forward to seeing you arrive home with an inventory full of achievements."

Miles had gasped. "Buckets of Bolts! To get that I'd have to defeat The Destroyer, The Twins, and Skeletron Prime, do you really think I can do that?"

Cedric nodded. "Of course. You can do anything."

Miles didn't want to disappoint his friends, but he also knew that this wasn't an easy task. He reminded himself that even if he didn't receive the Buckets of Bolts, his friends would still like him. They cared about him because of who he was, not what he achieved. As Miles thought about his friends, he spotted three new zombies lumbering toward him.

Miles fearlessly raced toward the zombies, slaying the first one with his sword and obliterating it. The other two zombies were stronger and trickier to battle. The bald zombies dripped with blood, and Miles tried not to stare at their gruesome faces as he struck the beasts with his sword. The zombie clawed at Miles with a disembodied limb, and the strike left Miles's energy very low. One more attack from the zombie and Miles would respawn in his bed.

Miles lunged toward the zombies, slamming his sword into their green flesh. He let out a sigh when both of the bald zombies were destroyed, and grabbed their two dropped zombie arms. He sipped a potion of healing to regain his strength and walked further away from his town. Miles knew he had to summon The Destroyer soon, before the night was over. If he just followed the instructions, soon he'd spawn this mechanical mob. Miles looked through his inventory, making sure he had all of the ingredients to summon The Destroyer.

"Rotten chunk," Miles remarked as he pulled it from his inventory. He remembered obtaining the rotten chunk when he defeated the Eater of Souls. Miles told himself that The Destroyer was no different than the Eater of Souls, which he defeated. Although he had Autumn by his side during that battle, he knew he could annihilate The Destroyer alone. Or at least he thought he could.

"Soul of the Night," Miles pulled out another ingredient needed to summon The Destroyer. He had obtained this drop when he defeated Corruptors. He knew all of these battles were helping him to prepare for this intense war with The Destroyer.

Miles needed one more item to craft the mechanical worm. He looked through his inventory, but it wasn't there.

Miles was irritated. "How am I missing a lead bar?" He paced as he looked through his inventory for what felt like the millionth time. His heart beat fast and his eyes swelled with tears. There was no way he'd be able to summon The Destroyer that night unless he was able to get his hands on a lead bar. He knew he'd have to mine for it, but he wasn't sure where he'd find a mine.

Walking further from home, he searched for a mine to gather his last item needed to craft a mechanical worm. Miles walked past trees thick with leaves, and saw a hole behind the bark of one of the trees.

"A cavern!" He exclaimed. "What luck!"

Miles sprinted toward the cavern, almost tripping over a chest that sat by the cavern's entrance. "This is really my lucky day." Miles opened the chest hoping to find a treasure, but the minute he leaned near it, he unleashed a piercing scream, "Oh no!"

The chest opened by itself. Miles jumped back as a large tongue protruded from the inside, and the chest leapt at Miles. It opened and closed like a mouth as it cornered Miles against the cavern's entrance.

"A mimic!" Miles screamed, clutching his sword. He looked up at three blocks that stood nearby. As he raced toward the blocks and climbed to the top, Miles wondered who had left them there. He grabbed a copper bow from his inventory and shot arrows at the mimic, but it wasn't losing strength.Miles hoped he had enough arrows to battle the mimic. He stood atop the blocks, and aimed the arrows at the mimic until it was destroyed.

"I can do this," Miles said as he slowly walked toward the cavern's entrance. He went down the stairs, and made his way into the dark and creepy cavern in search of a lead bar. He took a deep breath and as he walked inside, a giant bat flew past his head. Miles let out a yelp, and aimed his arrow at the winged pest that had flown too close to his head. The bat hid in the corner of the cavern. Miles ran his hand along the wall, trying to find it. He worried that the bat might be feral and its bite would destroy him. The cavern's wall was smooth and he wondered if the bat had flown out. Miles was about to put the arrow away and get his pick-axe when the bat flew past again. With one arrow, he skillfully destroyed the bat, picking up the coins it dropped.

When the bat was destroyed, Miles felt confi-dent enough to trade the arrow for a pickaxe. He walked farther into the cave, until he found a patch where he could mine for a lead bar. The success of his battles with the zombies, mimic, and bat helped Miles feel more confident. He was finally begin-ning to get used to being alone and enjoying the solitude. As he banged his pickaxe against the hard surface, Miles almost fell over in shock when he heard a voice call out.

Chapter 2:
I'M NOT YOUR GUIDE

"Are you my guide?" a man with red hair and glasses and wearing a green jacket, asked him.

"Excuse me?" Miles held his pickaxe. He knew he could use the pickaxe as a weapon if he needed.

"I'm Owen. Are you my guide?" the man questioned again.

"No, I'm not anyone's guide. And anyway, there are no guides in hardmode."

"What? I'm in hardmode? What's that? My guide Kyle never told me about it." He spoke rapidly, as if he was trying to get all of this information out in one breath. "I was defeating this crazy monster that had two bulging eyes and the sharpest teeth I've ever seen when all of a sudden I must have done something incredible because the crazy monster was gone and I landed here. I can't find Kyle anywhere. I just figured you were my new guide."

"I think you're talking about the Wall of Flesh," Miles said. "You defeated it. I hate to tell you this, but once you defeat the Wall of Flesh, you never see your guide again." Miles wanted to tell him about his own guide and how much he still missed him, but he thought it was better to stick to the basics.

"What? So now I'm in a totally new world? Where's Bunny?"

"Who's Bunny?" asked Miles.

"She's my friend and a serious party girl. She loves glitter and parties and having a good time. I even built her a house," explained Owen.

"If you built her a house, she's followed you to this world, along with anyone else you built a home for, with the exception of your guide. You'll just have to find her. Or she'll find you."

"Man, I'm going to miss Kyle. He was so smart. He taught me everything I know," Owen said, as two bats flew close to his head.

Miles shot an arrow at the bats, but missed. A bat flew past his head and Miles jumped back. As he fumbled with the arrow, Miles was ready to accept defeat from the feral bats. Miles backed away as he bat's mouth opened and it flew in for the bite. Miles closed his eyes, but nothing happened. He opened his eyes, "What happened? Where's the bat?"

"I destroyed it," said Owen.

"Where's the other bat?" asked Miles.

"I destroyed that one, too," Owen replied.

"Wow, impressive. Kyle must have been an amazing teacher," Miles said and pulled out his pickaxe, pounding at the ground.

"What are you looking for?" asked Owen. "And can I help?"

"That's nice of you, but I'd like to be alone." Miles didn't look up as he dug a hole.

"I want to work with you, can I? I'm very helpful. And you can be my unofficial guide."

"I'm not a guide, not even an unofficial one. I am trying to become a warrior, and this is something I have to do on my own," Miles wiped sweat from his brow.

"Don't you think it's easier to dig a hole with two people? I'm telling you, I'm very useful. I will help you become the best warrior. In fact, Kyle told me I'm a very good partner because I'm a great listener."

"If you're such a good listener, you should listen to my words." Miles enunciated each word rather slowly. "I don't need any help. I want to be alone."

Owen shrugged. "Okay, I know when I'm not wanted. Thanks for letting me know there isn't a guide in hardmode." Owen's tone was sarcastic as walked away and called out, "You've been very helpful."

"I'm sorry," said Miles as the hole grew deeper and he could only see Owen's feet. Miles spotted a chest near Owen. He watched Owen stand next to it. Miles screamed, "Don't open it!"

Owen didn't hear Miles. He reached down to open the chest, and cried out, "Help!"

Miles jumped out of the hole and sprinted toward Owen. Owen was battling the mimic, and within seconds he had annihilated the tricky mob.

"Wow!" Miles marveled. "You know you're an amazing fighter, right?"

"Am I?" Owen questioned. "I had no idea."

"Before you arrived. I was almost destroyed by a mimic. They are really hard to fight," explained Miles.

"So, do you want me to stick around?" Owen stood by the cave's exit.

"I have no idea why someone as skilled as you would even want to burden themselves with a partner," said Miles.

"I like having a friend. I get lonely on my own. Also, everything is better when you have more people involved."

Miles understood what Owen was saying, but he also knew that in order to grow, you had to go out on your own. This was a choice Miles had made, and he wasn't going to let this new person change his plans. Miles said, "You seem really awesome, but I want to be on my own."

Owen said, "I get it," and then paused. "Can I ask you why you're digging a hole? I'm really curious. Are you looking for buried treasure?"

"No," Miles chuckled, "nothing that interesting. I'm mining for lead. I need a lead bar to craft a mechanical worm to summon The Destroyer."

Owen pulled out a lead bar from his inventory and handed it to Miles. "I hope this helps you."

"Thanks, dude! This is awesome," Miles exclaimed. "Are you seriously just giving this to me? Do you want to trade anything?"

"Nope," Owen said. "You can have it. And good luck, okay? I hear The Destroyer is really fierce. Kyle told me many stories about mechanical mobs. They can be very lethal."

"Wow, I can't believe he told you about mobs, but failed to mention that he would be destroyed once you defeated the Wall of Flesh."

"I think he knew me really well, and that I'd never battle that crazy beast if I knew it would be the end of him," said Owen.

Miles remembered what a hard choice he had to make when he decided to battle the Wall of Flesh, and understood why Kyle never mentioned that fatal fact to Owen.

Miles held the lead bar in hand. The sun was going to come up soon, and he had just a short window of time to summon The Destroyer. He stared at the lead bar in disbelief. He couldn't believe how kind Owen was.

Miles said, "Owen, this means a lot to me. Honestly, I can't thank you enough. If you ever need help with anything, let me know."

Owen shook his head and mumbled something Miles couldn't make out. As Owen walked off in the darkness, Miles pulled out a pair of rocket boots and put them on to prepare for his battle with The Destroyer. The boots would give him the speed he needed to fight. Miles quickly crafted the mechanical worm, and summoned this mighty mechanical mob.

A message popped up alerting Miles that vibrations were shaking the world of Terraria. Within seconds a circular red-lit probe was shooting lasers as it flew toward him. Miles was struck by the lasers, and grew very weak.

"Help!" he screamed, suddenly hoping Owen was still in earshot, but nobody arrived.

As The Destroyer, the largest worm he had ever seen, lunged toward him, Miles had to battle this beast on his own. Despite his earlier protests, Miles realized he needed all the help he could get.

Chapter 3:
BAD NURSE

Miles wished he had wings. His rocket boots gave him some advantages—the speed and the height—but if he could soar up to the sky he was sure he'd defeat The Destroyer. There was no way around it; rocket boots weren't as good as wings. The long worm moved swiftly as it shot a never-ending shower of red lasers at him. Miles eyed the Destroyer, taking in the enormity of this mob, as he dodged lasers. When a laser struck his leg, Miles sipped a potion of regeneration as he shot the beast with his Palladium Repeater.

As another barrage of lasers flew in his direction, Miles jumped from the lasers with the aid of his boots. They made him run super fast, but it was useless; they weren't helping. He ran into another cluster of lasers, which weakened him.

The Destroyer unleashed a harsh clicking noise and the lasers set off loud explosions. Miles wanted to cover his ears, because he didn't like the piercing sound. Miles was both overwhelmed by the size and the noise emanating from this mechanical mob.

"Help!" Miles called out again. There was no response.

Miles was ashamed to admit, he regretted sending Owen away. Owen was right, it was easier to battle mobs when you had a friend by your side. Miles took another sip from a vial of potion, and realized it was empty. He had to annihilate The Destroyer quickly or he would be destroyed.

Three circular red probes detached from The Destroyer and circled around him. Miles jumped back. Two lasers flew toward him, striking both of his arms as the circular probes cornered him. Miles had to surrender. Could you even surrender to a mob?

It was at that moment that Miles remembered the magic mirror he had hidden away in his inventory. If he used this mirror, he would be able to transport home and escape from The Destroyer. Miles tossed his ego aside, and grabbed the magic mirror from his inventory, ready to go back home and be free from this enormous monstrous worm. Miles held the magic mirror, instantly transporting himself home.

It was nighttime and all of his friends were sound asleep. Miles paced the length of his small house, still energized from the aborted battle, but also extremely weakened. He needed help. At that moment, Miles heard a voice in the distance, and went out to investigate.

A woman wearing a nurse's uniform stood by a tree and Miles called out to her, "Who are you?"

"I'm Katie," she replied.

"Are you a nurse?"

"Yes, did my uniform give it away?" she asked.

"I'm very injured," explained Miles. "I was in the middle of a battle with The Destroyer and I was almost killed."

Katie inspected Miles's injured arms. "Quit complaining. I've seen a lot worse."

"But I'm in a lot of pain and I don't have much energy left." Miles was shocked at how easily Katie dismissed his injuries.

"What's your name?"

"Miles."

"Walk if off, Miles. You'll be fine."

"Okay, but do you have anything to help me?"

Katie searched through her medical supplies. "I can heal you. Do you have any coins?"

"Yes." Miles pulled out a bunch of silver coins and held them in his hand. "How many do you need?"

"Looks like you have enough." Katie helped herself to the coins and grabbed Miles's arm.

"Ouch!" he screamed.

"Does that hurt?" she asked.

"Obviously."

"Just what I thought," Katie replied.

Katie held her hand near his arm and his pain instantly disappeared. Miles was shocked and relieved to be pain free. "Thanks."

"Don't thank me, just build me a house," she said as she walked toward the village. "I want one of these nice ones, like all of these other people have. You built those, right?"

"Yes," Miles proclaimed proudly.

"Great, get started on it now," she demanded.

"But it's the middle of the night. We could be attacked by zombies," Miles rationalized.

"If we're attacked, I'll cure you. You've got more coins?"

"Yes," Miles replied.

"Then what's the problem?" Katie asked as she stood on an empty patch of land across from Miles's home. "Build it here."

"I thought nurses and people who work in the health care profession are supposed to be compassionate and understanding," Miles remarked as he grabbed supplies from his inventory and began to lay the foundation for the house.

"Where did you hear that?" Katie laughed.

"Everyone knows that," Miles replied as he carefully placed the blocks down, constructing the side of Katie's new home.

"Don't believe everything you hear," Katie said as she inspected the blocks. "Can you work any faster? I'm tired and I want to rest. It's the middle of the night, you know."

"I know." Miles finished one side of Katie's house as he kept a close watch for zombies.

"You can work faster, I know it," Katie berated Miles.

Miles didn't respond. He just completed one side of the house. He wanted to finish as fast as he could, because Katie was insufferable. He wondered what his friends would think of her. He hoped she'd be nicer to them, but he was doubtful.

As Miles worked on the house, a familiar clicking sound rang in Miles's ears. "What's that?" he shouted as his heart rate escalated.

"Oh no! It's The Destroyer," Katie spotted the red worm in the sky above the village. "And I'm stuck with the worst fighter in Terraria."

"That's not nice." Miles was upset by Katie's comment.

"Well, were you able to defeat it before?"

"Um, no," Miles confessed.

"Guess you have to do it now," said Katie.

"I wonder who summoned it," Miles said as he grabbed his Palladium Repeater and sprinted with his boots.

A red-lit probe flew at Miles. As he aimed his Palladium Repeater, he could hear the terrified screams from his friends when they saw what was happening and raced from their homes.

He had to defeat The Destroyer. He couldn't let this mob ruin his town. Miles struck the long belly of the wormy beast, as he heard a familiar voice call out, "Do you still want to do this on your own?"

Chapter 4:
TRY AGAIN

"**I** need all the help I can get," replied Miles.

"He certainly does," Katie screamed.

"Who's *that*?" Owen asked as he grabbed a pair of wings from his inventory.

"Don't ask. She's a nurse," replied Miles.

"Good, she can help us," said Owen.

"I wouldn't count on it," Miles remarked as he shot his Palladium Repeater at The Destroyer, shooting flaming arrows at the mob.

"Catch!" Owen screamed, and he threw a pair of wings toward Miles.

"Seriously? For me?"

"I have an extra pair. These are really awesome." Owen smiled as he lifted from the ground and, clutching his bow, flew toward The Destroyer.

Miles put the wings on. He wanted to enjoy flying with wings, which was the coolest thing he'd ever done, but he knew this wasn't about enjoyment, it was about saving his friends and village from an incredibly lethal mob. Miles could hear Katie screaming, "Fly faster. Destroy this beast, Miles."

Miles flapped his wings and dodged the lasers shooting toward him. Using his Palladium Repeater, he unleashed several flaming arrows at The Destroyer. The beast was losing energy, and Miles used his wings to reach the top of the enormous worm.

Although Miles was slowly making progress in the battle against The Destroyer, Owen was skillfully defeating this lethal mob. Owen flew around The Destroyer, almost taunting it as he tore into the mob with multiple arrows.

The Destroyer was infuriated and flew in the direction of the village homes. Its head banged into Katie's half-built home, knocking it to the ground. The beast aimed its rays at John the Merchant, who sprinted away.

"Stop!" Miles shouted at The Destroyer.

His friends called to Miles for help, but Owen was the one who fearlessly flew at The Destroyer and defeated the mob. The crowd cheered, and Miles joined Owen.

"Good job, Owen." Miles lowered himself to the ground and handed the wings back to Owen.

"Keep them." Owen made his way toward the ground. "They're yours now."

"First you give me a lead bar and now you're giving me wings. You're awesome, dude," Miles said, smiling.

Katie stepped between Owen and Miles, and yelled at Miles, "Quit talking, you have a house to build."

The sun came up as Miles's friends introduced themselves to Owen, thanking him for saving the day.

"It was nothing. I couldn't have done it alone," Owen said as he stared at Miles.

"I know nobody asked," Katie said, "but I'm Katie the nurse. Miles is building me a house."

"Okay, I'll work on it," Miles walked over to the rubble by Katie's house.

As he rebuilt the home, Sarah the stylist stood by his side, "I'm so glad you're back."

"I was only gone a day," Miles replied. "But I'll be honest, it seems like forever."

Owen walked over and asked if he needed help building the house. "I built one for my old teacher and guide, Kyle. He was really happy with it. I really miss him."

"Of course you can help." Miles handed blocks as he whispered to Owen, "The faster we finish this the quicker Katie will stop complaining."

"I heard that!" Katie called out.

John the merchant sprinted toward Owen, "You saved my life. I was going to be destroyed."

"I assume you're the merchant," Owen said. "I need to replenish a lot of my supplies."

"What do you need?" asked John.

"Almost everything. I'm going to get the Buckets of Bolts achievement with my friend Miles. I'll need supplies to beat both The Twins and Skeletron Prime," said Owen.

Miles stopped building the house. "I never said I would do that."

Owen stuttered, "I-I thought th-that we defeated The Destroyer, that meant we were going to be partners. I'm sorry if I misunderstood."

Cedric the wizard watched this awkward inter-action. "Maxwell?"

"Miles!" Miles corrected him.

Cedric looked down at his hand, "I'm sorry. I wrote your name on my hand and it was washed off. You know I'm bad with names. But that isn't important. I came over to tell you that there isn't any reason you shouldn't work with Owen. He's a fantastic fighter, and in the short time you've know him, he's also proved to be a good friend."

Miles knew Cedric was right.

"But I'm not sure I'm cut out to be a warrior," confessed Miles. "I was homesick the minute I left our town."

"I know what that feels like," Owen explained. "I can never go home. I'll never see Kyle again. Yet, I still want to become a warrior. I want to achieve the Buckets of Bolts. We only have to defeat The Twins and Skeletron Prime, and then we can come back as heroes. This was your original plan. Maybe you would have never done it on your own, but now that we've found each other, we can achieve this together."

Miles absorbed everyone's comments. "I can't do anything until I finish Katie's house."

"That's for sure," Katie added.

Miles walked back to the house silently. He constructed a wall of blocks as Owen joined him. "I don't want to force you to do anything you wouldn't want to do, but I think we make a great team."

"I know you're right," Miles said as he placed a door on Katie's house. "But I'm not certain I'm cut out for the life of a warrior."

"I think you are," said Owen.

Miles completed Katie's house. "It's ready, Katie. I hope you like it." Miles regretted saying those last words. He knew Katie was critical and she appeared to not like anything at all.

Katie walked inside the house, inspecting every area. "You know, I thought it would be bigger."

"Well, this is it," Miles replied.

Owen stood outside the house. "Will you promise me that you'll think about it?"

Miles nodded.

Chapter 5:
WE CAN BE HEROES

I t was still nighttime, and as everyone walked back into their homes, John screamed. "A zombie!"

"Where?" Owen asked.

John's shaky finger pointed to a shadowy figure shaded by leaves. "Over there," his voice cracked.

Miles grabbed his sword and raced in the direction of the bald-headed zombie. Owen followed closely behind him, striking the zombie at the same time as Miles did.

"We destroyed it!" Owen announced, and looked over at Miles. "We make a good team, right?"

"I guess so." Miles avoided making eye contact. He was still conflicted about Owen's offer to partner up. He just wanted to go home and sleep. This day felt as long as a year.

Miles started to walk back to his home, ready for bed, when Owen said, "I don't have a house. I don't have a place to sleep."

"I'll help you build one," Miles said, yawning.

"Don't worry, you're tired. I can build one." Owen stood on an empty patch of land that was the perfect size to build the house.

"I want to build it," Miles said. He wanted Owen to know that he still wanted to be his friend, even if he decided not to become his partner in battle.

Owen picked up blocks from his inventory and handed them to Miles. "Here, use these."

Miles shook his head. "I have enough supplies. You gave me the lead bar and wings. This is the least I could do for you."

Miles constructed the house, and when it was finished Katie walked over. "Hey," she said with a raised voice, "this house is much bigger than mine." Katie looked at Owen, asking him, "Can we trade?"

Miles replied, "No way. This is Owen's house."

Once everyone was safe in bed and the village was quiet, Miles fell asleep, but then woke up in the middle of the night. This had never happened before; usually he was a solid sleeper. He wondered if a sound had awoken him, but he as he sat up in his bed, he couldn't hear anything. It was absolutely silent. Miles wondered if his anxiety about giving Owen an answer was the culprit behind his sleepless night. Miles climbed out of bed and looked out the window. He spotted two zombies in the distance. He wanted to wake Owen and ask him to help him destroy these beasts, but instead, he sprinted from his house, ready to battle the zombies on his own.

The two zombies lumbered toward Miles, and he surprised himself when he struck them both and almost instantly destroyed them.

A voice came up behind them. "Good job."

"Owen," Miles said, surprised. "I didn't know you were here."

"I couldn't sleep and I saw you battling the zombies," said Owen.

"I wasn't sleeping either. I don't know what to do," confessed Miles.

"I have an idea. Why don't we summon The Twins tomorrow? If you don't enjoy that battle, you can come back to the village. If you do enjoy the victory of defeating the pair of creepy eyes, we can go spawn Skeletron Prime," suggested Owen.

Miles thought about Owen's suggestion. "Okay," Miles responded. "That sounds like a good plan." It would be the first time they would be working together from the outset.

"Perfect." Owen was excited. "In the morning, we must prepare ourselves for the battle."

Miles went back to his house, and was completely shocked when he instantly fell back to sleep. He didn't wake until morning when he heard Owen knocking on his door. "Are you up?"

Miles groggily crawled out of bed and called out, "Almost. Come in."

Owen smiled and handed Miles a strip of bacon. "You have to eat. We need our strength to battle The Twins tonight."

Miles sat on the edge of his bed, taking small bites of the crisp and tasty bacon. "Wow, this is really good. How did you know bacon was one of my favorite foods?"

"Everyone loves bacon, right?" Owen laughed.

"Do you have a strategy for the attack on The Twins?" asked Miles.

Owen's arm waved as he spoke rapidly. "Well, I figure The Twins are just a trickier version of The Eye of Cthulhu, which I destroyed quite easily. I don't think this is going to be a hard battle at all. It's not like when we annihilate The Golem."

"Slow down. I just promised to battle The Twins, remember? I didn't sign up to battle The Golem. That would mean we'd first have to destroy Skeletron Prime and Plantera. Can we take it one step at a time?"

Owen sighed. "I know, but I have so many ideas and plans. I can't wait to battle The Twins. I wish it was nighttime already."

Jack the Demolitionist walked into Miles's house. "Need any explosives?" he asked.

Miles was annoyed. "Haven't you ever heard of knocking?"

"Sorry," Jack replied, "but I'm having a going out of business sale and I had a bunch of stuff I wanted to unload."

"You're not going out of business," Miles retorted.

"Okay, I'm not," confessed Jack, "but I do have a lot of useful items for you."

"Funny," Owen said. "You must have read my mind. We need to get some parts. We are going to craft a megashark."

"Wow," exclaimed Jack. "That's an intense piece of weaponry."

"My old guide Kyle once handed me a shark fin and told me that one day I'd need to craft the megashark when I attack The Twins," explained Owen.

Miles was constantly impressed by the knowledge Kyle had imparted onto Owen. "You really think the megashark is powerful enough for us to defeat The Twins?"

"Yes, and I have some strategies too," Owen paused. "For instance, we have to focus on defeating the Retinazer first."

"You really sound like you know what you're talking about. I'll just follow your lead," Miles said as he took his last bite of the bacon. John knocked on the door and Miles told him to come in. "See?" Miles said and eyed Jack. "John has manners."

John asked, "How's everything going? I heard you guys are summoning The Twins. Are you nervous?"

"More excited than nervous. I love the idea that we could be heroes. I mean, in just a matter of days, we might have the Buckets of Bolts achievement. It's like a dream," Owen said, smiling.

John pulled out an iron anvil and an assortment of healing potions. "Do you need any of these?"

Miles said, "We need it all. Especially the healing potions. I'd rather use those than have Katie help me."

"Um, hello," Katie said, coughing, and letting herself in. "You don't have to be so rude. When you're in bad shape, you'll wish I was by your side."

"I didn't mean to be rude," Miles apologized. "But I also have to ask everyone to leave. Owen and I have to start crafting the megashark now. We don't have that much time to get ready for battle."

Sarah stood by the open door. "Before you start building anything, I think Owen needs a haircut."

"Really? I do?" Owen was surprised.

Miles looked at Owen's long red hair. "Don't take this the wrong way, but she might be right."

Sarah cut Owen's hair while Miles set up the crafting station in the corner of his house. As he placed each on the crafting table, he teemed with excitement. Owen's haircut was finished and Miles gave him a thumbs up.

"I think we're almost done with the megashark." Owen looked at the crafting station.

"Now we have to craft the most important item," said Miles. "The mechanical eye."

Without the mechanical eye, the duo wouldn't be able to summon The Twins. As evening approached, Miles looked through his inventory, hoping they had all of the necessary items.

Chapter 6:
I'VE GOT MY EYES ON YOU

"Do you have a lens?" asked Owen.

It was the final item needed to craft the mechanical eye. Miles searched through his inventory. "I know I have it somewhere. I picked one up after destroying a demon eye." Yet no matter how hard he searched he couldn't find it.

"You must have it your inventory. Just slow down and you'll find it."

Miles hoped Owen was right. He would be very upset if he had misplaced this essential component. "Okay, but I don't see it."

"We have to find it soon," Owen said, looking out the window. The sky was getting dark, and they wanted to travel far outside of the village before summoning this vicious mob. Owen didn't realize how close he was to the village when he summoned The Destroyer. It wasn't until after the battle was over that he understood the devastation

The Destroyer could have caused upon the village. They were lucky that Katie's half-constructed home was the only thing to be ruined. Lives could have been lost. Owen was glad it ended well, and knew that in the future, he'd conjure up the mobs far from the village.

"I'm looking, but I'm telling you it's not there," Miles said, panicked.

"Can I look?" asked Owen.

"Be my guest," said Miles.

Owen searched through Miles's inventory. "I found it!" Owen exclaimed.

"Really? How?"

"I guess you kept passing over it." Owen pointed to the lens. Miles extracted it from his inventory, and within minutes they were holding the mechanical eye.

"I think you should carry it in your inventory," said Miles.

"Good idea," Owen agreed.

"Are we ready?" asked Miles.

"Think so," Owen said, and smiled.

"I'm not going to lie. I am really nervous," confessed Miles.

"Me too," said Owen, clarifying, "in a good way. I'm excited for this adventure, but it's normal to be nervous."

The duo emerged from Miles's house, greeted by all of their friends. Autumn the mechanic rushed over with Isaac the tinkerer. She wished them well. "I just want to say that Isaac and I are so excited to hear all about your adventures when you come back."

Miles looked back at his house. He didn't want to disappoint his friends, and he hoped he wouldn't come back to tell them that he was destroyed and simply respawned in his bed. He wanted to come back a hero.

Owen said, "We will come back victorious, or at least we will try to come back as heroes."

The friends waved goodbye as they trekked into the forest and the sky grew dark. After they walked a few miles, Owen asked, "Do you think we're far enough away from the village?"

Miles was very protective of his friends. "I don't think so. I want to be really far away."

"But we have to summon The Twins before the sun comes up," said Owen.

"I know," Miles said, "we will, but I just want to travel a bit further from the village."

The duo walked for another few miles, Owen was worried the sun would come up in the middle of their battle. "I think we are far enough. Let's summon The Twins," he said, pulling the mechanical eye from his inventory.

Miles was shaking as Owen summoned The Twins. Suddenly a message appeared telling them it was going to be a terrible night.

"Oh no!" Miles cried, as the two incredibly gross eyes spawned in front of them. "They're right! This is a terrible night."

"Don't focus on how gruesome the eyes are, just take out your megashark and shoot!" instructed Owen.

With sweaty hands Miles grasped the megashark and shot, but it didn't hit either of the two eyes. "Help!" Miles screamed, as purple lasers shot from the Retinazer.

"Don't forget, we have to destroy the Retinazer first," Owen shouted as he grabbed the megashark and aimed it at the Retinazer.

"The other eye," Miles cried, "it's also a mouth!"

"That's the Spazmatism," Owen screamed. "Just avoid it. We have to destroy the Retinazer first."

Miles couldn't avoid the Spazmatism—it was chasing after him. Every few seconds the bulbous eye opened and shot green flaming balls at him. He was struck by one and quickly drank a potion of healing. He didn't want to admit this, but he wished they had brought Katie with them on this adventure. Miles was inches from the Retinazer, when Owen screamed, "Shoot!"

Miles aimed the megashark at the Retinazer and blasted the eye until it disappeared. Miles was thrilled at his achievement, but the joy was short lived when he looked over and spotted his friend Owen having a hard time battling the Spazmatism. Miles put on his wings and flew toward the Spazmatism, shooting at the mouth-like eye. He skillfully destroyed it. Miles lowered himself to the ground and picked up the Soul of Sight, which The Twins had dropped.

Owen let out a deep breath. "Thank you. You did it, you defeated The Twins."

Miles handed some of the Soul of Sight to Owen. "We did this together."

"But really, you were the one who destroyed The Twins."

"You're the one who told me what to do," Miles replied, smiling.

As the sun rose Owen said, "We just made it. If we didn't destroy The Twins a minute ago, the battle would have been over because of the sun."

"I'm just relieved we don't have to summon The Twins again. That was intense," said Miles as he drank a potion to regain the energy he lost during battle.

"I think we should head back to the village," suggested Owen. "We need to replenish our supplies if we want to battle Skeletron Prime tonight. We're going to have to craft a mechanical skull."

Miles was energized from the defeat, and said, "You're right. Let's battle Skeletron Prime tonight, and by tomorrow, we'll have the Buckets of Bolts achievement and will be noted warriors."

"Wow, I thought for sure I was going to have to convince you to battle Skeletron Prime."

"No, you're right. We make a really good team. I'm ready for the next battle."

"That's awesome!" said Owen.

As they made their way back to town, Miles suggested, "Why don't we put our wings on and fly back to town?"

The two started to soar up into the sky, when a voice called from below, "I like your gear."

Chapter 7:
THERE'S NO STOPPING US

Miles lowered himself to the ground and took off his wings, "Who are you?"

"I like your wings, but I have something way cooler," said a woman wearing a hat.

"Really? What?" questioned Owen.

"Who are you?" asked Miles.

"So many questions!" she said and laughed.

"Well, are you going to answer them?" Miles was annoyed.

"I'm Hope," she said, smiling. "I'm a steampunker and I have lots of cool items I can sell you, but first you have to do one thing for me."

"Is that to build you a house?" asked Miles.

"That's right!" Hope exclaimed. "I bet you've done this before, right?"

"A lot," replied Miles. "There is a village, where a bunch of NPCs live."

Owen added, "You'd like it there."

"I'm sure I would. Can you lead me there?" asked Hope.

"Yes," replied Miles.

"On the way, I'll tell you about what I can sell you. I see you guys like to fly, and I have a jetpack I could sell you guys," said Hope.

Owen exclaimed, "What? Seriously? I want to buy it right now." He grabbed a bunch of coins from his inventory. "How much does it cost?"

"I want one too. I hope you have two," added Miles.

"Yes, I do." Hope took the two jetpacks from her inventory and they both handed her coins for their new jetpacks.

Owen slipped the jetpack on. "This is like the coolest thing ever."

Hope said, "It's also very useful when you're in battle."

Miles put his jetpack on and flew next to Owen. "This is awesome!"

As they flew an orange glow spewed from the jetpack, and Miles pointed at the orange fumes. "What's that, Hope?" he asked.

"Don't worry, that's normal. However, I think you guys should come down. Didn't you promise to build me a house?"

Owen and Miles landed next to Hope. Miles smiled. "That was intense. What other cool things do you have?"

"I'm not showing you anything until we get to your village," Hope declared.

The duo led the way. "I will build you a big house," Miles said as they approached the town. "You just have to promise to sell us something as cool as that jetpack."

"We're almost there," Owen said. He could see the rooftops of the homes. Owen had only just met Miles's friends and settled in the village, but he already felt like he was returning home.

Sarah was the first person to greet them. "What happened?"

"We destroyed The Twins," said Owen. "And tonight we will defeat Skeletron Prime."

"Wow, you're busy guys," remarked Hope.

Hope introduced herself to everyone as Miles and Owen worked on her home. Katie watched them, commenting that Hope had an extra window and even had room for a throne.

"The sun is going to set soon." Owen looked up. "We have to craft the mechanical skull."

Miles looked through the list of items. "Bones, Soul of Light, Soul of Night, and lead bars."

Standing by the Orichalcum Anvil in the corner of Miles's home. Owen searched through his inventory and reported, "I think we have everything."

The duo crafted the skull. Once they were done Miles held the skull. "Is there anything we can't do together? Honestly I feel invincible."

"Me too," said Owen. "Together we're unstoppable."

Miles said, "I can't wait to defeat Skeletron Prime. Do you have any strategies?"

"I know we can defeat it by just killing its head. That sounds easy, but it isn't. I think with the jet-packs or the wings, we have a shot at destroying it. I'm feeling very good about this battle."

"Me too. Is it almost nighttime?" asked Miles.

Owen walked to the window to see if the sun was setting. He stood by the window transfixed at what he saw and didn't reply.

"What's wrong? Do you want to put on the jet-pack and go for a quick ride before we leave?"

"No," Owen replied in a monotone voice as he stared out the window.

"Is there a problem? Two seconds ago you were so excited to battle Skeletron Prime. What changed?"

"Come over here," Owen replied.

Miles walked over to the window, and stood next to Owen. He was speechless as he looked out at red sky.

Chapter 8:
UNDER A BLOOD MOON

"I guess we can't summon Skeletron Prime tonight." Owen looked up at the blood moon, which illuminated the sky with a rose-colored tint.

Blood-curdling screams echoed outside Miles's door. "Oh no! We have to help our friends!" Miles bolted from his house, clutching his bow.

Outside of Miles's door, standing in front of his friends, was a red nosed clown carrying an item with a smiling face.

"It's just a clown," Miles said as he looked for the usual suspects that spawned during a blood moon, like the zombie bride and groom, those eternally wed destructive creatures of the night. Miles eyed the clown. "It's just carrying a balloon, I think."

"That's not a balloon!" cried Owen.

The clown laughed maniacally as it tossed the yellow-smiling-face ball into the air and it exploded steps from Katie.

"This clown is going down," Katie hollered as she grabbed a handful of poison needles and aimed it at the clown. One of the needles landed on the clown's arm, but he brushed it off.

Miles shot an arrow at the clown, as the green-haired jester aimed another smiling bomb at them.

"Use the jetpack," Hope called out. "It will give you an advantage."

Miles jumped back, avoiding the bomb that exploded in front of him, and pulled the jetpack from his inventory. He pressed a button and lifted off. Hovering above the clown, he was able to shoot two flaming arrows that struck the strong clown. Miles wondered what they needed to do to destroy this laughing clown, as he pounded it with two more flaming arrows. He spotted two corrupt bunnies hopping toward Autumn and Isaac. Miles called out to them, but they couldn't hear them. He looked down at the clown. It stood directly below him, and Miles knew this was the ideal spot to attack the clown, but he had to fly over to Autumn and Isaac and stop the lethal bunnies.

Owen fumbled with his jetpack; he finally lifted off into the air towards Miles.

Miles pointed as he passed Owen. "C'mon, fly over there. See the bunnies?" Miles flew as fast as he could, calling out to Autumn and Isaac, "There are bunnies behind you."

Autumn threw a wrench at the bunnies, hitting one of the corrupt ones, but it still hopped in their direction. Isaac lovingly and sacrificially shielded Autumn from the bunnies, as he quickly threw a succession of spiky balls at the cute but seriously corrupt bunnies. The spiky balls destroyed one of the bunnies, but the other bunny hopped faster and lunged toward Isaac. Autumn pushed Isaac away as she aimed two wrenches at the bunny, destroying it.

Isaac sighed. "Those bunnies were hard to destroy."

"I know," cried Autumn as she stared off in the distance. "It looks like they have lots of friends."

Isabella and Sarah noticed the cluster of bunnies hopping toward the village, and joined Autumn and Isaac in the battle. Sarah leapt at the bunnies with her scissors, while Isabella crafted a leaf barrier around three bunnies, trapping them as she zapped them of their energy.

"Look at the new bunch of bunnies," Owen called out to Miles as they battled the clown alongside Cedric, John, and Katie.

"That's their challenge. We have to destroy this tricky clown, because his bombs are extremely deadly," Miles called out as he shot what felt like the millionth flaming arrow at this indestructible clown, but still couldn't destroy it.

Miles and Owen were both on the ground, and the clown was inches from them, taunting them with the smiling-faced bomb.

"I have no idea which direction he is going to throw that bomb," Miles whispered to Owen.

No matter how many poison shots Katie threw or knives John unleashed or fireballs Cedric aimed at the festively dressed fatal joker, it only weakened him, but didn't destroy him.

The clown laughed even louder than before as he tossed two smiling face bombs in opposite directions. Miles closed his eyes as he shot a flaming arrow, and then heard two loud explosions. When he opened his eyes, the clown was gone. "Did I destroy it?"

There was no response. Miles looked for his friends, John, Cedric, and Owen, but he didn't see them. He told himself that it was nighttime and it was harder to see people. Miles rushed through the village, looking for his friends and hoping they weren't destroyed by the clown's bomb or even worse, from its flaming arrow. Miles frantically called out to his friends who had helped battle the clown with him.

Then finally he heard Sarah cry for help. "Miles! We need you! There are too many bunnies! Come here!"

Miles didn't know which direction he should go—all of his friends needed help. *If only the blood moon hadn't occurred*, Miles thought to himself. *We'd be summoning Skeletron Prime right now, instead of being in big trouble.*

Chapter 9:
TOTAL ECLIPSE OF THE HEART

"Miles," Owen called out. "Over here!"

Miles let out a sigh of relief when he spotted his three other missing friends. "What happened?"

"We were hiding from the clown," said John.

"I think you destroyed it," added Owen.

"Yes," Miles said, "it's gone. But my eyes were closed, so I have no idea what happened."

"You shouldn't aim with your eyes closed," Owen reprimanded him.

"I know," Miles confessed, "but I was just scared."

"Well, closing your eyes isn't going to work," said Owen.

"It looked like it did," Katie said.

John looked off in the distance at the others. "They need our help with the bunnies!"

Sarah's voice was louder and tinged with fear as she cried, "Help!"

Isabella was slowly weakening the trapped bunnies within her leaf barrier, but there were scores of other bunnies hopping around the village. Miles destroyed two with flaming arrows, but every time someone destroyed a bunny, it seemed like more instantly spawned in front of them.

"These bunnies multiply fast!" Isaac said as he threw two more spiky balls at group of bunnies. One of the balls landed on a bunny's back. Miles shot a flaming arrow at that weakened bunny, destroying it, before it could lunge at him.

Owen looked up at the sky. "Don't worry guys, it's almost morning, and the bunnies will all disappear. We don't have too much longer to battle them. Let's try to stay alive."

"I'm trying!" Miles said as he leapt from the bunnies that surrounded him.

The sun rose, and one by one the bunnies disappeared.

"It's over," Owen announced and everyone cheered, until Miles called out, "Not quite."

"What do you mean?" asked Owen as the sky turned dark. He didn't need an answer. "A solar eclipse!"

The gang was exhausted from their night battling the vicious clown and corrupt bunnies under a blood moon, and now they were stuck with a rare solar eclipse.

"I feel like we're cursed," Isabella cried.

Miles eyed the area for any hostile mobs, spotting Frankenstein in the distance. This ironically energetic zombie mob that only spawned during a solar eclipse was much faster than a regular zombie and even harder to defeat. Miles grabbed the jetpack and his bow and flew toward Frankenstein. Owen flew next to him.

"This is intense," Owen exclaimed as he shot two arrows at Frankenstein, but the arrows barely damaged this super zombie. With perpetually outstretched arms, the zombie leapt at Isabella, who stood below Owen and Miles. Isabella skillfully captured Frankenstein within her leaf barrier, as she worked hard to weaken the beast.

Sarah let out a piercing scream when she saw a ghoulish figure dripping with water standing behind her. "Help! What is that awful thing?"

Owen flew over to Sarah, striking the swampy creature with a succession of arrows that ripped through the watery flesh, destroying it. Owen lowered himself to the ground and picked up a broken hero sword it dropped. "That's a swamp thing. It must have come from the murky swamp waters that are nearby. They're very common during a solar eclipse."

Hovering above them in the sky, Miles saw three swamp things lumbering toward the town. "You're right. It looks like more swamp things are heading this way."

Owen screamed at Miles, "Watch out! Next to you!"

A bat flew toward Miles. "A bat!" he cried as he flew away from it and steadied himself, aiming his bow at the bat.

"It's not a bat!" Owen called out. "Destroy it fast! It's a vampire."

The bat flew closer to Miles. He tried to strike it with an arrow, but it was impossible. The bat bit Miles. "Ouch!" he cried before he disappeared from the dark sky.

"Miles!" Owen screamed as he saw the gravestone flash across the sky. Owen looked like he didn't know which direction to go. The bat was advancing toward him, and the swamp things were walking through the center of the village. Plus, another Frankenstein might spawn. As the bat flew toward Owen, it transformed into a gruesome caped zombie, inflicting Owen with the bleeding debuff and removing his last bit of energy. Within seconds, Owen had respawned in his bed.

Owen grabbed a bottle of potion and took a quick sip to regain strength. Climbing out of bed, he sprinted into the village, ready to seek his revenge on the vampire, but he was too late. Miles was pounding the gape-mouthed vampire with flaming arrows, annihilating the beast. Owen sprinted toward his friends, who were battling the swamp things.

With Owen by his side, Miles was able to save their friends from the clutches of the creepy swamp things. Miles scanned the area. "It looks like the mobs might be gone for now."

"You spoke too soon," Owen cried as a sea of bats flew toward them.

Autumn threw as many wrenches as she could, yet only one struck one of the bats. The bats landed, morphing into vampires.

"I wish the sun would come up!" said Miles.

"Me too!" John cried as he threw knives at the vampires, knowing he was no match for these blood-sucking mobs.

Miles knew they were outnumbered and even the jetpack wasn't going to help them. He needed to think of something that could save them, and he had to do it fast. Miles quickly put on a pair of lightning boots, and used his advantage of speed to annihilate two vampires.

"Only five more to go," Owen said as he put on his pair of lightning boots and destroyed two more vampires.

"We're almost there!" Miles looked over at his partner. He was happy he wasn't in this alone. His NPC friends were able to fight, but none of them would ever be as strong as another warrior.

"Yes, we are!" Owen was ready to destroy the rest of the vampires. The victory of defeating the two vampires filled him with hope. He knew they could win this battle, but they just had to keep their energy up.

Katie suddenly moaned, "Frankenstein, and he has a twin friend!"

Owen signaled to Miles that he could finish up the vampire battle on his own. But just then, Miles was surrounded by two Frankenstein monsters, and their extended arms created a box around him. Miles was trapped.

Chapter 10:
LIFE IS A PARTY

Miles reached for his arrow, but the Frankensteins simultaneously leapt toward him. Miles was about to close his eyes when a flaming arrow destroyed one of the Frankensteins and Owen called out, "Get the other one, dude!"

Miles shot a barrage of flaming arrows at the Frankenstein, destroying it. Sarah sprinted toward them, pointing at the sky. "It's over! The solar eclipse is over."

Two broken hero swords were dropped by the mobs and Miles picked them up, handing one to Owen.

Owen looked up at the sky, and let out a sigh of relief when he saw a normal moon as evening approached. "I'm so glad that we don't have another blood moon tonight."

Miles said, "Now we can summon Skeletron Prime. The mechanical skull wasn't damaged, was it?"

Owen checked his inventory, and unearthed the mechanical skull. "No dents. It's ready to go."

"But maybe we should wait another day," Miles said. He didn't realize how fatigued he was from the battle, and he wanted to be alert when they summoned this deadly mechanical mob.

"Really? You want us to wait an entire day? You must be kidding. Let's do it now. I want that Bucket of Bolts achievement."

Miles remembered his first battle with Skeletron before he was in hardmode. He was destroyed by the devilish mob, because he was overeager to battle him. He knew he needed rest, but he just had to convince his friend. "I want to spend the day mining for supplies, and getting prepared for the battle."

Owen placed the mechanical skull back in his inventory. "We have everything we need, what is your problem?"

"You battled Skeletron before, right?" questioned Miles.

"Of course," replied Owen.

"Did you get it on your first try?"

Owen paused. "Well, no."

"I think this is going to be a lot harder than the original Skeletron, and I just want us to be prepared, but we can leave tonight if you want."

"Great, let's go. It will be nighttime soon, and . . ." Owen didn't finish his sentence, because someone walked into the village and called out his name.

"Owen, sweetie," called a girl with red hair like Miles's. She appeared in the center of the village and raised her voice. "You abandoned me."

"Bunny," Owen pleaded, "I couldn't find you." He looked over at Miles, "Didn't I tell you about Bunny the party girl?"

"Yes," confirmed Miles. "We were looking for you, but there were so many battles and Terraria is so large, we never found you.

"What about me?" asked an older man with gray hair who wore a big red-rimmed hat and trailed behind her.

"Who are you?" questioned Miles.

"I'm Roland. I'm Owen's clothier."

"You never told me about Roland," said Miles.

"I forgot." Owen regretted saying this, because Roland looked down glumly.

"You forgot about me?" Roland asked.

"No, I'd never forget you, but I just didn't mention it to Miles," Owen explained and then asked Roland, "Do you have any new clothes for me? I'd like to buy some."

Roland took out a clown suit. "I just started selling this. I think it's quite popular. You only get to buy it when someone destroys the clown. So it's a sign of success."

"That outfit gives me the creeps," said Katie.

"I appreciate your honesty," Roland said, looked at Katie. "But I'm trying to make a sale here, so can you just mind your own business?"

"Roland, this isn't the time to sell anything," said Bunny. "Unless anyone wants a super cool confetti gun."

"I guess you're right," Roland said. "We are not here to sell, but to ask you to help us."

"How? I'll do anything for you guys. I owe you a lot," Owen said.

"Can you build us new homes?" asked Bunny. "Now that Kyle is gone, it was just us in the middle of nowhere. I couldn't throw any parties and obviously being in the middle of nowhere meant that nobody was inviting me to any either. It's just awful there. Can't you build us homes here, so we can have friends?"

Roland added, "I just want to be near you. I'd live anywhere if it isn't too far away. I'm not looking for a party, but if you happen to be going to a party, I have a great suit I can sell you."

"Of course I'll build you homes here," Owen said and looked at his other friends for confirmation. He realized this wasn't just his decision alone, and he had to ask everyone else if it was okay if these new people stayed.

Everyone agreed that Owen should build homes for Bunny and Roland before the sun set. Miles helped as Owen crafted two homes next to Katie's house.

"Seriously? You're going to block my view?" Katie was annoyed.

Miles and Owen didn't listen to Katie's complaints as they built the homes. Bunny stood by them, marveling at the construction. "This place is going to be super awesome. I can tell already."

Owen stared at the one wall of blocks he had constructed. "I'm glad you think that, but we've barely started."

Bunny talked endlessly about how she was going to decorate the house. "Lots of sparkles, tons of glitter, a disco ball is a must."

"Sounds like I'm going to have some noisy neighbors," Katie remarked.

"No, I'm quiet as a mouse. I'm a tailor. I just like to work on clothes. Maybe I can design a new nurse's uniform for you?" asked Roland.

"Don't bother," she replied, and asked Owen and Miles, "Can you also build a fence?"

Bunny laughed, hoping Katie was joking as she stood next to Owen asking him a series of questions. "So what are you up to these days? Have you slayed any beasts? You destroyed the clown, right? Any reason for me to throw you a party? You know I throw the best parties, right? They are epic, right?"

"Yes, you do throw a bunch of good parties," Owen said as he placed a window on Bunny's house. "And there will be reason to celebrate soon, because we're going to defeat Skeletron Prime and get the Buckets of Bolts achievement."

"Really? Once you get that, I'm totally going to throw an after-party for you, okay? Like a seriously fun one? Everyone cool with that?"

John confessed, "I've never been to a party, that sounds like fun."

"Well, you're in for a treat. Even if you've been to other parties, they are nothing compared to my parties. I throw the craziest parties in the world."

"Wow, you're so humble," Katie said, then walked toward her house.

When Katie was out of earshot, Bunny said, "I know she's going to have the most fun at my party. The ones who complain are always the first ones to admit my parties are the best. You'll see, after a few weeks of living next to me, that nurse is going to be a lot more fun."

"Don't hold your breath," remarked Miles as he finished Roland's house.

Roland walked inside his new home. "This is great. There's enough room for me to set up a work area to make clothes. I'm back in business. Thanks!"

Miles looked up at the sky, "Owen, I was thinking we should leave now that the sun has set, so we have enough time to travel far way to spawn Skeletron Prime.Or maybe we should just leave in the morning."

"I guess leaving in the morning is a good idea," said Owen.

Miles was relieved; he had another night to sleep in his own bed. "Great. We'll leave in the morning."

"Yes, we don't want to waste any valuable time traveling all night, because if we don't defeat Skeletron Prime by morning, we'll have to respawn it."

"Do we even have enough supplies to craft another mechanical skull?" asked Miles. "Do we need one?"

"I'm not sure," said Owen as he searched through his inventory.

"Do you need a confetti gun?" asked Bunny. "It makes battle fun. I mean who doesn't want to sparkle a little fun into their fights?"

Miles chuckled and replied, "You've sold me. I'll take one."

"And how about this clown hat with embroidery? I guess you can call it a party hat. It complements the confetti gun."

"Okay," said Miles. "You can embroider 'Miles' on the hat." He looked at Bunny and said, "I'll wear it to the after-party once we defeat Skeletron Prime."

"That better be a promise," Bunny said and smiled.

Roland took out the hat, and started to embroider Miles's name. It took a rather long time. Miles stared at the sky. "We should all get to bed soon, Roland. Owen and I have to wake up early and leave, but I don't want to rush you."

"I think embroidery is difficult," said Owen.

"Of course it is! If it wasn't hard, no one would do it! That's what makes it great," Roland said as he handed the clown hat to Miles.

"That's how I feel about defeating Skeletron Prime," Miles said and thanked him for the hat.

"You will both have many challenges during the battle, but don't give up. Even if it looks like there isn't a chance to win, there is always another way," Roland told them.

They said goodnight and in the morning, Owen stood at Miles's door, ready to go. Jack was next to him. "Remember," Jack said, "we're here if you need us. I have tons of explosives that will destroy Skeletron Prime."

"I know," said Miles.

"And don't forget about your jetpacks." Hope rushed over to say goodbye.

As Miles and Owen walked out of town, they could hear Bunny's voice, "Guys, we have to get ready for this after-party. I want it to be a blow-out event. Now, where's that stylist? We speak the same language."

Chapter 11:
HARD LUCK IN THE HALLOW

"It feels like we've been walking forever," said Miles. "My feet hurt."

"I think we're in a good spot to summon Skeletron Prime," Owen said. "We just have to wait until dark."

"Look at that!" Miles pointed at a brightly lit area in the distance. It looked like it was pulled from the pages of a book of fairytales. The trees' leaves were purple and yellow, with turquoise grass, making it look like a colorful, picturesque land. Miles had been there before. "It's The Hallow," he said. "It must be growing over there."

"Kyle told me about The Hallow. He said I should be careful because it wasn't as fun as it looked. In fact, he said it was quite the opposite."

Although Miles and Owen stood still, The Hallow didn't, and within minutes the leaves on the trees that surrounded them turned from green to a pinkish purple. "Looks like we didn't have to travel to The Hallow, because it came to us."

"Look, a unicorn," said Owen.

"They're very dangerous," warned Miles.

"But they look so gentle."

"Watch out!" Miles hollered. "Put your bow away, and use the Dao of Pow."

The unicorn charged toward them, jumping over blocks, as Miles shot from the Dao of Pow, which struck the unicorn and left it confused.

"I don't have that weapon," Owen screamed.

"The unicorn is confused. This is our time to escape. Follow me," Miles said as he rushed through The Hallow, hoping it would end soon, but it felt like a never-ending biome. Miles remembered Isabella telling him The Hallow was growing rapidly and had already taken up thirty-five percent of the world. Miles swore he'd stop the growth of The Hallow like he did with the Corruption.

Owen shouted, "Above us! What's hovering above us?"

"Pixies!" Miles informed him.

Small flickering lights swarmed above them. Miles put on his jetpack and shot arrows at the fast pixies that flew toward them.

"I'm getting attacked!" Owen could barely get these words out as the pixies cornered him. He was losing energy.

Miles took out the megashark and slammed into the pixies, destroying a group. Even wearing a jetpack, Owen was having a difficult time fighting the Pixies. They moved quickly, and struck Owen with the slow debuff. Owen cried out, "I can't move."

Miles aimed at the pixies that flew toward Owen. "I'm going to help you!"

"Behind you!" Owen cried.

Miles turned around, and saw the unicorn charging in his direction. With a swarm of pixies in front of him, and an aggressive and muscular unicorn behind him, Miles wanted to close his eyes, but he knew that wasn't a solution. With his eyes wide open, Miles used the megashark to destroy the pixies and turned around and aimed at the unicorn. The megashark annihilated the unicorn in one shot.

Owen's slowness wore off and he grabbed the megashark, attacking the pixies that circled around with their flickering light.

Miles and Owen grabbed the dropped pixie dust and unicorn horn.

"We have to get out of this biome," Miles exclaimed.

"I know. It's almost nighttime," Owen replied. "But how?" Owen looked at another group of pixies that flew toward them. Miles hovered above the ground, transfixed by the beauty of the pixies.

Owen caught him staring at the light and screamed "Pay attention. They are going to destroy us."

Miles pressed the button on his jetpack and flew toward the light-filled pixies, as another enemy spawned on the ground. "Look down," he called to Owen. "What is that?"

Owen lowered himself. "It's made of slime," he said, inspecting the red circle on the ground, when it began to hover and shoot a laser at him.

"Watch out for that Gastropod!" a voice called out.

Miles's jaw dropped when he saw his friend *Asher* sprinting toward them. Asher promptly shot the Gastropod using a megashark.

"Man, thanks!" Owen said as he watched the Gastropod disintegrate.

Asher wore wings and flew toward Owen, helping him battle the pixies that surrounded him.

"It's been a long time," Miles said when the final pixie was destroyed.

When Owen heard that, he was shocked. "You guys know each other?"

Miles and Asher nodded.

"Why didn't you tell me you had such cool friends?" asked Owen.

"He's not that cool," Miles said, staring at Asher.

"I thought we put all of that behind us. I've been slowly destroying the Corruption. See how much Purification Powder I've used?" Asher took out the remainder of his Purification Powder from his inventory and showed Miles.

"Okay, I see you've proved that you've changed. And everybody deserves a second chance," said Miles.

"What happened?" Owen was curious.

Miles replied, "It was nothing. It's in the past and it's going to stay there." He introduced Asher, "This is Asher. He's an old friend. And this is Owen, he's my new friend."

Chapter 12:
OLD FRIENDS AND ENEMIES

There was no time to go into Asher's back-story, as four Gastropods spawned on the ground, and another unicorn charged at them.

Asher said, "I know how we can get out of here."

Miles aimed at the unicorn and struck the side of the horned animal. Asher took another shot, delivering the fatal blow.

"Just shoot at the Gastropods," Asher screamed at them. "And follow me."

"Should we?" Owen asked Miles.

"What, is he your boss? Do what *you* want," shouted Asher.

"We should follow him," said Miles.

They shot at the Gastropods as they made their escape from The Hallow.

"When we get out of here, we're summoning Skeletron Prime," said Owen.

Miles was annoyed that Owen revealed their plans. Asher might have sprayed Purification Powder throughout the world, saving Terraria from the Corruption, but he had a past. Asher had blown up Miles's village. He held his tongue, however. Miles didn't want to taint Owen's image of Asher.

"Skeletron Prime," Asher said. "I've beat him. I know the best tricks."

"Really? What?" Owen sprinted next to Asher, listening carefully to every word that came out of Asher's mouth.

"Yes, I did it on my own. I'm not going to say it's easy. It took me a few times, and the most annoying part was crafting that mechanical skull."

"We already have that," said Owen.

Miles wanted to shout at Owen that he was telling Asher too much, but he didn't and he was boiling with rage.

"We're almost out of The Hallow, and since it's night, we can spawn it when we leave," Asher informed them.

Miles didn't like the way Asher immediately included himself in their battle with Skeletron Prime. Again, he didn't say anything.

"Miles, you've got to keep shooting the Gastropods or we'll never get out of here. Also don't stop looking for pixies, they come out of nowhere and they will slow you down," Asher called out to Miles.

"Thanks for the tips," Miles's comment was tinged with sarcasm, and Asher picked up on it.

"I was only trying to help," said Asher.

"Are we almost out of The Hallow?" Owen wanted to summon Skeletron Prime, and he was getting antsy.

"We should be, but it keeps growing, so I'm not sure," said Asher, "but once we are, we'll waste no time using that mechanical skull and summoning Skeletron Prime."

"Great," Owen said without even looking back at Miles "This is going to be amazing. I'm going to battle Skeletron Prime with an expert. That's priceless."

Miles felt invisible as he aimed his Megashark at the unicorn that leapt at him. He cried for help, but he was fairly certain they wouldn't turn around and help him. Asher and Owen were far ahead of him, talking about Skeletron Prime. Miles angled the megashark at the unicorn, but he couldn't hit the white muscular animal. He called out, "Help!"

"Just fly fast!" Asher yelled. "We're almost there!"

Miles could see the end of The Hallow, and Owen screamed, "Not again!" Miles flew as fast as he could to escape the unicorn and find out what was going on. He was barely an inch away from the unicorn when he flew out of The Hallow.

"Miles," Asher said, "it's a blood moon."

"I know. We just had one," Miles said.

"We can't summon Skeletron Prime," Owen remarked as he destroyed a corrupt bunny.

Miles was still carrying the megashark and used it to destroy a blood zombie. Asher instructed, "You don't want to use that on zombies. It's a waste of ammunition."

Miles knew Asher was right, but it still annoyed him. It also bothered him that Owen clung to Asher's every word, and treated him like a sage.

"Wow, you remind me of my old guide, Kyle," said Owen. "I really felt like he knew everything."

Miles destroyed four corrupt bunnies and a zombie bride, but Owen didn't notice or ask him for any tips.

What looked like a red fish with bulging eyes appeared in the sky, as Asher screamed, "Dripplers! Duck!"

Owen put his head down and asked, "What next?"

"They don't move fast, so you can destroy them with a sword. You have a sword, right?" asked Asher.

Owen took out his sword, lifting himself in the air with his jetpack and swung at the Drippler, destroying it "You're right! I got one!" Owen exclaimed.

Miles stood face to face with a zombie groom when he accidently dropped his megashark, leaving him defenseless. "Help!" Miles shouted, but nobody heard him.

Chapter 13:
GOALS

Miles tried to pick up the megashark, as the zombie groom lunged at him. Standing behind the groom was his veiled bride, who advanced toward Miles. He called out for help as he leaned over to pick up his megashark, leaving him exposed and vulnerable to the married zombies. The zombie groom stood less than inch from him when Miles grabbed the megashark and aimed it at the couple, instantly destroying them.

"Didn't I tell you not to waste your megashark ammunition on zombies?" Asher called out.

"Where were you when I needed help?" screamed Miles.

"Sorry, I was helping Owen battle the Dripplers," Asher replied.

"He was," Owen confirmed.

"Aren't you going to pick up the wedding veil and the top hat they dropped?" Asher walked over to the dropped items, and Miles grabbed them before he could pick them up.

"Next time I'm outnumbered by zombies, can you guys help me?" asked Miles.

"If I'm not in the middle of another battle," replied Asher.

Owen was about to say something, but paused as five blood zombies stomped toward them. Blood oozed from their bright red bodies and their bulging yellow eyes glared in their direction.

"Blood zombies!" Owen cried.

"We have this," Asher said. "Just follow me."

Asher pulled throwing knives from his inventory and threw them at the blood zombies, piercing the skin of two of them. Asher wasn't pleased with his results. "I think this is better suited for the job," Asher said, pulling out a long spear. He swung it at the blood zombies, striking three of them. "Now that's much better."

Owen followed Asher and used throwing knives to defeat the blood-dripping enemy. Miles used a sword to strike the zombies, destroying one after a few blows from his sword.

"We destroyed them." Asher looked over at Owen.

"What is that spear? I've never seen it before," asked Owen.

"It's a Vilethorn. I was lucky to get it when I destroyed a shadow orb in the Corruption. It's magic," explained Asher.

"Wow," marveled Owen. "What other weapons do you have?"

"The key to battle is not about the weapons you have, but understanding how to use the weapons, and knowing which one is the best for that fight," Asher said as he pointed toward the sky. "More Dripplers. Use your sword, Owen, and strike them."

Owen struck the Dripplers as they hovered above them. Miles stood by Owen, striking the red flying beasts with his sword. Every time Owen destroyed a Drippler, Asher cheered. As the sun came up. nobody seemed to notice Miles had destroyed two Dripplers on his own.

"It's a new day," Owen said as they stood in the middle of the jungle. "It was so dark and I was so fixated on destroying the enemies that spawned during a blood moon, I never realized we were in the middle of the jungle."

"I wonder if there is a jungle temple around here," Asher said.

"Asher, if you've defeated Skeletron Prime, I bet you have the Buckets of Bolts achievement, don't you?" asked Owen.

"I didn't want to brag," Asher said, "but yes, I do,"

"That's my ultimate goal," said Owen, "and if there's no blood moon tonight, I am going to achieve that goal."

"We both are," added Miles. "We're partners."

Owen confirmed, "You're going to fight Skeletron Prime, right Asher?"

"I've defeated Skeletron Prime, and I told you, it's very tricky. But I think my knowledge will be quite useful in battle. I will be there."

"Great, I think you're going to be very helpful. I'm so glad I met you." Owen smiled at Asher. "And after I defeat Skeletron Prime, I'm going to defeat Plantera and The Golem and --"

"It sounds like we have the same goals," Asher said, interrupting. "I want to defeat all of those enemies too. I want to be a great warrior."

"I thought you were selflessly spreading Purification Powder around Terraria to stop the growth of the Corruption," remarked Miles.

"I'm the ultimate multitasker; I can do both. I've defeated Skeletron Prime and stopped the Corruption from growing. Ask Isabella; she knows a large percentage of the Corruption has been shrinking, thanks to me. In fact she's personally thanked me. People don't have to stick to just one job. They can have multiple goals."

"I guess that's true," said Miles. "I'm just glad your goals don't involve burning down innocent people's homes anymore."

"Anymore?" questioned Owen. "What does that mean?"

"It's nothing," Miles said. "I shouldn't have brought it up."

"No worries," Asher said, smiling. "I know I've done some bad things in my past, but I am making up for it now."

Owen asked, "Have you ever defeated Plantera? That's my ultimate dream. I mean Buckets of Bolts is great, but once you defeat Plantera, you get a temple key."

Asher looked down as he spoke. "No, I haven't. I've tried, but I can't seem to destroy it."

"I'll help you defeat it. Once we conquer Skeletron Prime tonight, there's no stopping us, Asher," Owen said, "I have the mechanical skull in my inventory, and we have the entire day to plan our strategy of attack."

Asher rattled off various attack plans and facts, "As you know Skeletron Prime has four limbs, and destroying the head will kill him, so you have to focus on the head."

"I thought there are five parts to Skeletron Prime," said Miles.

"There are. The head isn't a limb. I just said four limbs and a head. Weren't you listening?" Asher was annoyed.

Miles added, "Doesn't standing on a platform give us an advantage? Shouldn't we build something?"

"I thought I mentioned that already," said Asher. "Owen, do you have wooden platforms in your inventory? We can hammer them to those stairs." Asher pointed to stairs near an old abandoned village. "That old village is a great place to summon Skeletron Prime.We can construct platforms there, and also shield ourselves behind the rubble from the old homes."

The four homes clustered together had an eerie feel. "I wonder who used to live here," remarked Owen.

"I don't know, I assume they found a new place to live," said Asher as he stopped by the stairs. "Okay, let's start building the platform here."

Owen and Asher grabbed supplies to construct a platform. Miles handed them a wooden platform, but Asher said, "Don't worry, we have it covered."

"We make a great team, don't we?" Owen looked over at Asher.

Miles cringed as he heard Asher reply, "Yes, we do."

Chapter 14:
THE ATTACK OF SKELETRON PRIME

The sky grew dark as Asher paced and reviewed the game plan. "We have to stay focused and take this battle seriously. We can't slack, okay Miles?"

Miles had no idea why Asher thought he was the weak link. "I don't know why you'd think I'm going to slack during the battle, when I was very helpful battling The Destroyer and The Twins, right Owen?"

"Yes, but we have to listen to Asher. He's defeated Skeletron Prime. He's an invaluable resource," Owen replied and asked Asher to continue going over various strategies.

"I know you guys have jetpacks. Use them," said Asher.

"What about wings?" asked Owen.

"Everything is helpful. You can use wings, too. Also the Dao of Pow is extremely useful, do you have one?" asked Asher.

"I do," said Miles.

"I don't," said Owen.

"Hmm, maybe you should lend Owen your Dao of Pow," suggested Asher.

Owen stared at Miles as Miles responded, "But then what will I use?"

"No time to go into any great details now." Asher looked up at the dark sky. "There's no blood moon. Let's summon the beast. Owen, where's the skull?"

Owen carefully took the mechanical skull from his inventory and placed it on the ground. "Should I summon it now?" His voice shook.

"Yes," Asher replied.

Standing on the platform, dressed in Palladium armor, Owen, Asher, and Miles crowded around the mechanical skull as Owen summoned the most potent of all three mechanical bosses.

Miles shook as he stared at Skeletron Prime's blinding red eyes and gaping tooth-filled mouth.

"Miles, now is the time to use your megashark!" screamed Asher.

Miles picked up his megashark as Asher hollered that he should aim for the head. Asher had already destroyed one of the four limbs that floated in the air.

"You got the prime saw!" Owen called out.

Miles jumped back from the clutching fist, also known as prime vice, one of the remaining three limbs. Each limb contained a different weapon. One shot lasers, and Miles tried to dodge a laser attack, but he was struck. His energy level was low, and he quickly sipped a potion to regain his strength.

"Shield yourself," Asher called out to Miles.

Asher and Owen stood side by side as they aimed at Skeletron Prime's head, and Asher warned Owen every time he was too close to a limb. "We're going to do this, buddy. Just keep aiming at the head."

Miles couldn't aim at the head, as he was cornered by prime vice. The fist clutched toward him, and he used his jetpack to fly from the menacing hand. The minute he flew into the sky, the limb with the lasers shot at him, hitting his foot. Miles grabbed another potion. As he took a sip, he wondered if he'd lose this battle, while Owen and Asher would come back to town as heroes.

"Why aren't you using the megashark?" Miles could hear Asher shout, but he was soaring high in the sky, and getting too close to Skeletron Prime's limbs.

"Lower yourself," Owen screamed.

Miles heard Asher say, "Owen, let's not worry about him. He's going to make us lose this battle."

Skeletron Prime's head began to spin and grow spikes as it headed in Miles's direction. "Help!" Miles shrieked.

Chapter 15:
STRENGTH IN NUMBERS

Miles was struck by a fireball from prime cannon. "Ouch!" he cried, grabbing his arm as he raced from the spinning head. His jetpack was losing steam and he couldn't fly any higher. Miles lowered himself close to the platform, where Owen and Asher were slowly weakening Skeletron Prime's spinning head. As he reached the wooden platform, prime vice charged at him, clutching onto one of his legs. He couldn't break away from prime vice's grip. He wiggled and shot prime vice with the megashark, but it was impossible to escape; he was trapped.

Owen aimed his megashark and struck prime vice, but Asher told him to focus on the head. Owen didn't listen. Instead, he flew toward Miles, annihilating prime vice and saving his friend.

Owen flew back to Asher, as Miles regained his strength and navigated the jetpack toward the head. He wanted to destroy the head so Asher would see he was a skilled fighter. He would be the first to admit that he was having issues in this battle, but he wanted to conquer Skeletron and obliterating the head was the best way to do it.

Prime laser shot a death laser at Miles. He flew from its rays, but wasn't fast enough. The laser landed on his chest, inflicting damage. Miles grabbed a potion of healing, gasping when he realized this was the last potion in his inventory. He sipped the potion and continued to fly in the direction of Skeletron Prime's spinning head.

Prime cannon flew in his direction and he circled around the arm, avoiding its fireball. Miles was learning how to avoid attacks from the various limbs, but he also knew that attacking the head was a bold mission. If he didn't destroy Skeletron Prime's head, he would be the one that was destroyed. He had no potions to help him recover. He had to destroy the spinning head fast. Miles used his jetpack to fly close to the head.

As he approached the spinning skeleton head with large red eyes, he could hear Owen cry out, "Stop! That's not a good idea!"

"Are you crazy? Don't get too close. It's spinning!" Asher called from the safety of the platform.

"I'm going to destroy it," Miles said as he blasted the head with his megashark, but the head still spun toward Miles, and he knew this was the end. He could endure one strike from the spinning head, but with two strikes he'd be a goner. The head spun toward Miles and struck him. He flew away from the head, but it trailed behind him. Miles's megashark wasn't weakening the bony head and he knew he didn't have the energy to last much longer.

Miles was about to close his eyes, when he saw Asher fly towards him. As Asher flapped his wings, he aimed the megashark at the spinning head, "Don't worry, I've got it." Asher said quite confidently.

The spinning head was inches from Miles; he was too weak to hold his megashark and it dropped onto the platform, leaving him defenseless.

"Oh no!" Owen cried. "The sun is coming up! Get that head now Asher, or we'll have to battle it again."

Asher flew past Miles, handed him a potion of strength and gave him instructions. "Use your Dao of Pow and help me defeat this head."

Miles quickly sipped the potion, and grabbing his Dao of Pow, he flew next to Asher and they sprayed the spinning head with projectiles that led to the demise of Skeletron Prime.

"You did it, you guys destroyed Skeletron Prime!" Owen exclaimed.

Chapter 16:
BUCKETS OF BOLTS

Before the sun rose, Miles and Owen were rewarded with the Buckets of Bolts achievement. As the sun came up, they stood in the middle of the jungle.

"Should we spawn Plantera tonight?" asked Asher.

"Can't we just enjoy getting this achievement? I know you already have one, but this is a big deal to us," Miles explained. "Everyone back home is going to be so proud of us."

"I can't believe I have the Buckets of Bolts achievement," said Owen.

Miles stared at Asher. "I can't believe you saved my life."

"Believe it." Asher smiled.

"You guys destroyed Skeletron Prime together," added Owen.

Asher said, "We all did it. And now we're going to battle Plantera."

Miles confessed, "I'm glad we were able to defeat Skeletron Prime together, but I have to admit that ever since you guys met, I feel like a third wheel. You both have so much in common, and I feel like I just don't belong."

"I'm sorry you feel that way," Owen said. "I didn't realize this."

"Really? We went from being partners to me be becoming invisible," said Miles.

"I was just excited to meet Asher. He had already battled Skeletron Prime and he reminds me of Kyle. He's always teaching me how to become a better fighter, which is my ultimate goal."

"Maybe I just don't share the same goals as you guys," said Miles.

"I will admit that I might have been a bit rude," Asher said, taking a deep breath. "But as you know I am trying to become a better person. I don't want you to feel left out. We really needed you when were in the middle of the battle. I know we're seriously going to need you when it comes time to battle Plantera. That plant is intense."

Miles shook his head. "It's hard when there are three people, and I think someone always feels left out."

Owen asked, "But can't we be The Three Amigos?"

"Yeah, that's perfect, The Three Amigos battle Plantera. It sounds like the name of a super awesome movie," said Asher.

"It does," Owen agreed.

"Listen, if we're going to battle Plantera tonight, we've got to be prepared. Let's sort through our inventories to make sure we have the proper supplies. I know we were running low on potions, and Owen doesn't have a Dao of Pow. We can head back to my house and start crafting weapons and potions. I don't live too far from here."

Owen looked in his inventory. "I'm running low on a lot of supplies. I might have to go mining."'

"We better start making a list of everything we need," said Asher.

"Good idea," Owen said as he listed a bunch of supplies they needed to battle Plantera.

"What do you have in your inventory, Miles?" asked Asher.

"Um," Miles said as he looked. "I'm all out of potions."

"I can help with that," said Asher.

Miles was conflicted. He did enjoy his new friendship with Asher, and knew he wouldn't have been able to defeat Skeletron Prime without him and Owen, but he also felt like he was being forced into something he didn't want to do. Miles had to speak up.

"I don't know if I want to be apart of The Three Amigos. I want to go home. I miss my friends and

I would rather tell them about defeating Skeletron Prime than running off to battle Plantera," Miles explained. "I just want to go home."

Owen said, "Maybe going back home is a good idea. We can get a bunch of supplies from everyone there. I know Jack has explosives and I need to replenish my supply."

Asher paused. "Miles, do you think everyone will be okay with me coming back to the village?"

"What did you *do* to the village?" Owen asked.

"As we said before, it's in the past," explained Miles. "I think they will be happy to see you. Isabella would love to hear how you're stopping the Corruption. I'm also sure Sarah would want to give you a haircut; you've definitely let your hair grow."

"Let's go back to the village," Asher said.

"Don't forget Bunny is going to throw us a cool after-party. Bunny throws the craziest parties," remarked Owen.

"Who's Bunny?" asked Asher

"She's a friend of Owen's, and a party girl," said Miles.

As they walked toward the village, Asher spotted The Hallow in the distance. "We want to avoid going back through The Hallow."

Miles saw a man standing outside of The Hallow painting a picture of the biome. "Who is that?"

Asher looked at the man. "I have no idea, I've never seen him before."

Owen approached the man, "What are you doing?"

"Can't you see I'm painting?" replied the man, who was wearing a red beret and holding a paintbrush.

"It's a really nice picture of the Hallow," Miles stared at the painting. "You really captured the colors. Especially the turquoise grass."

Without looking up from the painting the painter said, "I know the difference between turquoise and blue-green. But I won't tell you."

"Don't worry, we won't ask," said Asher.

"What's your name?" asked Owen.

"Carlo, and yours?"

"Owen, and these are my friends Miles and Asher," said Owen.

"Owen, can you do me a favor?" asked the painter.

Owen smiled. "Do you want me to build you a home?"

"Are you a mind reader?" Carlo was shocked.

Owen laughed. "No, I've just seen this before. Of course, come back to our village with us."

"We're about to go to a party in our village," said Miles.

"Those party girls really paint the town red," Carlo said. "That sounds like fun. I'll paint a picture of it for you."

"I'd like that," Miles said, as they tried to avoid The Hallow. But no matter how they tried to avoid it, they couldn't get around The Hallow. Miles stared at the rainbow overhead, and braced himself for another trip through his brightly colored challenging biome.

With one foot in The Hallow, Miles screamed as a unicorn charged at them. Carlo splattered the unicorn with paintballs. Asher threw knives at it, as Owen and Miles used their bows, until the unicorn disappeared.

"After conquering Skeletron Prime, this trip through The Hallow is going to seem like a breeze," said Asher.

"I hope you're right," Miles hollered as a sea of pixies flew in their direction.

Chapter 17:
CHOICES

As the pixies surrounded them, the trio shot arrows at the flickering lights emanating from the yellow creatures of The Hallow.

"We destroyed them all," Asher said gleefully. "See how well we work together?"

"You guys are like The Three Amigos," said Carlo.

"I know! We are!" exclaimed Owen.

Miles knew he had to make a choice. Although they worked well as a team and ironed out all of their issues, he knew he didn't share the same interests. His friends were motivated by achievement, and Miles was motivated by the thought of sleeping in his own bed, and not in a strange place in the middle of a jungle or a snowy biome. Miles couldn't wait to get back home and out of The Hallow.

"Watch out!" Owen warned them as two unicorns sprinted in their direction.

Miles hid behind a purple tree, and watched as Owen and Asher battled the unicorns. He told himself that they'd be fine without him, and they could be the Deadly Debonair Duo rather than The Three Amigos. He hoped they'd understand that he wasn't going to join them in the battle or Plantera after they returned home. But he wasn't sure they would. He had already tried to tell them, and they didn't listen.

Another unicorn sprinted through The Hallow. This time Miles couldn't hide behind a tree, and Asher called to him, "Miles, get the unicorn. You don't have any potions left. You can't get hurt by it."

Miles aimed at the unicorn, destroying it with a single shot. Owen raced over to him. "You're such a great fighter. I'm so glad to team up with you. We are totally going to defeat Plantera."

Asher gave Miles a high five, and Miles felt a pit in his stomach. "Thanks," he said quietly.

"Look, there's an exit," Owen pointed to the end of The Hallow. As they sprinted toward the exit, Carlo's screams echoed through the pastel colored biome.

Two pixies hovered above Carlo; he feebly threw paintballs at them, which didn't weaken the pixies.

"Help!" Carlo cried.

Miles used his jetpack to soar next to the pixies and strike them with his sword, destroying each of them.

"How can I thank you? Can I paint you a picture?" asked Carlo.

"Let's just get out of The Hallow safely," Miles said as he sprinted out of the colorful biome and toward his village.

Chapter 18:
AFTER PARTY

"They're back!" Sarah called out.

Owen exclaimed, "We did it! We got the Buckets of Bolts achievement!"

"*Asher*?" Isabella asked, "Where did you find him?"

Asher replied, "They found me in The Hallow. I've followed your directions and have destroyed much of the Corruption."

"I know," remarked Isabella. "We are grateful to you for doing this. Do you need any more Purification Powder?"

"I can definitely replenish my supply," said Asher.

"Purification Powder! Boring! Let's get the disco ball rolling! I want to party!" Bunny raced into the center of town. "Now that you guys have the Buckets of Bolts, I am throwing you the best party ever. First we will feast on Pad Thai and after that we will dance until dawn."

"They must build me a house before you begin your marathon night of partying," Carlo said.

"I promised to build him a house," Owen explained.

"We'll help." Asher looked over at Miles, who nodded his head that they would help him construct the house.

"Can you just give him Bunny's house?" Katie asked. "I can't deal with her anymore. She plays music all the time."

"I bet if you danced more, you'd be a happier person." Bunny shot Katie a dirty look.

"I'm building it here," Owen stood by a patch of land near trees and a mountain, "On the edge of the village, so Carlo will be inspired and paint pictures every day."

"Thank you," Carlo said. "I couldn't ask for anything more. What a lovely idea."

"Better build it fast!" Bunny exclaimed. "The party starts soon. It's at my place. I have a disco ball."

Owen finished the house alongside Miles and Asher. Carlo entered his new home, excited about the large picture window. "This place is perfect. Now go off to your party, you guys deserve it."

Asher said, "We can't stay long if we want to get to the underground jungle to see if Plantera's bulbs have grown."

Miles knew he had to tell them that he wasn't going with them, and that The Three Amigos were over. "I'm sorry, guys," he said.

"Sorry about what?" asked Owen.

"I can't battle Plantera with you. I want to stay here. I hope you'll understand," Miles said tearfully. "I know you guys are going to become the best warriors in Terraria. I can't wait to hear about all of your adventures, but I can't participate in them."

Owen sounded heartbroken. "I'll miss you a lot."

Asher said, "Me too. I was really getting used to the idea of The Three Amigos."

"I've renamed you. I think you guys could be the Deadly Debonair Duo," Miles told them.

"Hmm, maybe we can remove Deadly and just be the Debonair Duo," suggested Owen.

As they walked into Bunny's party, Miles put on his embroidered clown hat, and their friends greeted them with cheers. Owen announced, "I'm afraid this is also a farewell party. Soon, Asher and I will travel to the jungle to defeat Plantera."

"Miles, are you not joining them?" asked Cedric.

Miles was excited Cedric got his name right. "Nope, I'm staying here."

Asher added, "For now, right? You never know when we'll need your help."

Miles smiled. "If you guys really need me, you know I'll always be there."

Bunny raised her voice. "Quit yapping and start dancing."

The music played and Miles couldn't have been happier, as he twirled underneath the disco ball with his friends. Out of the corner of his eye, he could see Carlo standing beside an easel painting a picture, immortalizing this moment that Miles never wanted to forget.